The Careless Kitten

About the story

The little kitten rushes around like a mad thing, getting into trouble and causing havoc wherever she goes, fast using up her precious nine lives.

The Careless Kitten

There was once a madcap of a kitten. It just simply didn't care what it did! It leapt here and it leapt there, it ran up the curtains, it hid under the bed, it got between people's feet and tripped them over.

The kitten's mother lived next door and was always hearing tales of the madcap kitten of hers.

"Do you know, the kitten jumped into the pond today!" cried the big dog. "Splash it went! It was after the goldfish, silly little thing."

"And will you believe it, it

scratched the big dog up the road,"
chirped a sparrow. "*Scratched* it!
Well, if the kitten hadn't leapt up a

tree at once it would have been bitten to bits! It won't last long at that rate."

The kitten's mother was very worried. She spoke to the dog. "That's twice the kitten has almost lost its life," she said. "Twice! It's only got seven lives now, and it's hardly four months old."

"Seven lives left – what do

you mean?" said the dog.

"Well, didn't you know that all cats have nine lives?" said the cat. "I suppose you poor dogs only have one. Well, we have nine – and I'm so afraid my kitten is using hers up too quickly. Once nearly drowned – once nearly bitten by a dog – that's two lives gone in a week."

"I'll warn her," said the dog. But

before he could say anything the kitten climbed up to the roof of the shed and fell right off it to the ground! The dog ran up to see if she was in bits – but no, she leapt up and ran off, laughing at the dog.

"That's three lives gone!" called the dog. "Come here, I want to talk to you."

But the kitten was cheeky and ran away. The dog watched for her, and saw her in the road the very next day. He ran to tell her what her mother had said but before he could reach her the little thing ran straight out into the road. A car came along and the kitten disappeared under it.

"Well – it will be killed for certain," thought the dog. But no, it came out from under the car

as frisky as ever. Not one of the wheels had touched it.

"Hey! That's four lives gone!" barked the dog. "Will you please come here, you silly little thing! I've a message from your mother."

"I don't want to hear it," mewed the kitten. "Mother's always scolding me. Go away."

She ran up a tree and the dog couldn't get near her. He barked at the bottom. The kitten ran down, patted him on the nose and ran off in front of him. He ran after her, determined to make her listen. But she ran straight up a tall telegraph pole, to the very, very top!

And, of course, she couldn't get down! When she tried to she lost her balance and fell – right on top of the surprised dog!

He tried to grab her in his mouth, but she was off again at once. "Listen! That's *five* lives gone!" barked the dog anxiously. "Do, do listen to me."

But the kitten wouldn't. She ran into the house and the dog couldn't follow.

A week later he saw the kitten again. She was prancing about round a horse's hooves. Down came a hoof on the kitten's tail, just missing the little thing's head.

"Another life gone," groaned the dog. "Only three more left. She'll have lost them all before I can warn her about them."

Then the kitten lost two more lives very quickly indeed. She jumped up on a pile of books and they all toppled over on her, almost squashing the life out of her tiny body – and in a great fright she rushed up to the bathroom to where Sammy, the little boy, was having a bath, and jumped straight into the hot water to be with him!

Mother brought down the kitten to dry her in the sun. She was wet through and frightened. Mother put her down by the big dog.

"Look after the poor little thing for me," she said. "She's nearly killed herself by overbalancing a great pile of books and then by leaping into

Sammy's hot bath-water. Get a little sense into her head, Rover."

"Eight lives lost," said the big dog, and he licked the kitten gently. She was very, very wet.

"What's all this you keep saying about lives being lost!" she said.

So Rover told her. "You've got nine lives, like any cat – and you're throwing them all away, one by one. You've lost eight of your lives already. You've only got one left to last you now. What are you going to do about it?"

"Goodness why didn't somebody tell me this before!" said the kitten in alarm.

"I shall be very, very careful now. I shall lose my silly ways and grow into a sensible, well-behaved cat."

So she did – and everyone said, "Oh, what a pity it is that kittens so soon grow up and lose their playful ways and turn into solemn sedate cats."

Well, now you'll know why they do – it's because somebody suddenly

tells them about their nine lives, and
they decide not to waste any more!
How many lives has *your* cat had?
Mine's had about seven already.

About the Storyteller
Enid Blyton

Enid Blyton wrote poems, stories and plays to amuse herself as a young girl, and after training as a kindergarten teacher she had her first book published.

In all, Enid Blyton wrote around 700 books, including The Famous Five, Malory Towers, The Magic Faraway Tree and Noddy.

Today, her books are available in more than 40 languages and films, television series, video and audio cassettes, CD ROMs and other merchandise, ensuring that she remains the world's favourite children's author.

About the Illustrator
Sylvia A Ward

On leaving school at 15, Sylvia joined County Studio as a trainee illustrator. Over the years she has developed her style of work to include licensed properties for American and UK publishers as well as greeting card and gift wrap designs.

She has designed and produced patterns for Tiffany style stained glass panels. Her hobbies include hand engraving glassware in her own style and design, also collecting curios.